The Dressing-Up Box

Written by Mairi Mackinnon

Illustrated by Kate Sheppard

How this book works

The story of **The Dressing-Up Box** has been written for you to read with your child. You take turns to read:

You read these words.

I'd like to be a mermaid.

4

I can sit
on a rock.

Your child reads these words.

You don't have to finish the story in one session. If your child is getting tired, put a marker in the page and come back to it later.

You can find out more about helping your child with this book, and with reading in general, on pages 30-31.

The Dressing-Up Box

Turn the page to start the story.

I'd like to be a mermaid.

I can sit
on a rock.

Or maybe a circus acrobat –

I can get up
on top.

Perhaps I'll be
an artist.

I can pick
up a pen.

Or how about a
grizzly bear?

I can dig a den.

I'd like to sail the
seven seas.

I can mop
a deck.

Or watch me score
the winning goal –

I can kick
at a net.

I could be an explorer.

I can pack
a map.

Or maybe a sleeping princess.
Hush now!

I can nap.

Perhaps I'll be a superstar chef?

I can pick
up a pan.

I can be anything I like,

I can,

I can,

I can!

Puzzle 1

Match the speech bubbles to the pictures.

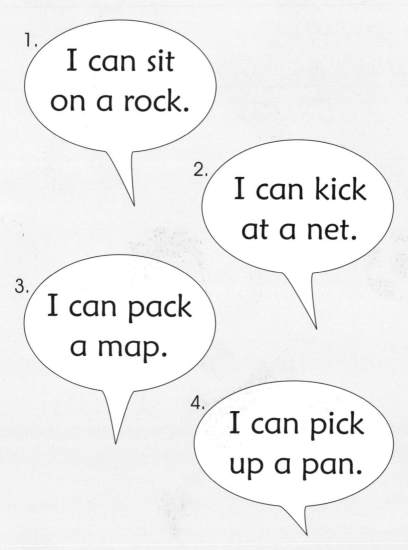

Puzzle 2

Choose the right word to complete the sentence.

1.

I can get up on ....

mop	pop	top

2.

I can .... up a pen.

kick	lick	pick

3.

I can mop a ....

| deck | dock | duck |

4.

I can ....

| nag | nan | nap |

Puzzle 3

Look at the pictures, read the sentences, then say whether they are true or false.

1. **I am a cat.**

2. **I am sad.**

3. **I am sick.**

4. **I can kick.**

Answers to puzzles

Puzzle 1

1. I can sit on a rock. – D
2. I can kick at a net. – A
3. I can pack a map. – B
4. I can pick up a pan. – C

Puzzle 2

1. I can get up on <u>top</u>.
2. I can <u>pick</u> up a pen.
3. I can mop a <u>deck</u>.
4. I can <u>nap</u>.

Puzzle 3

1. True
2. False
3. False
4. True

Guidance notes

Usborne Very First Reading is a series of books, specially developed for children who are learning to read. In the early books in the series, you and your child take turns to read, and your child steadily builds the knowledge and confidence to read alone.

The words for your child to read in **The Dressing-Up Box** introduce these eight letters or letter-combinations:

(Note that in this story, c, k and ck all have the same sound.) These are often among the first letters that children learn to read at school. Later books in the series gradually introduce more letters, sounds and spelling patterns, while reinforcing the ones your child already knows.

You'll find lots more information about the structure of the series, advice on helping your child with reading, extra practice activities and games on the Very First Reading website,*
www.usborne.com/veryfirstreading

*US readers go to **www.veryfirstreading.com**